Dear Client

By

Eddie J Martin

Acknowledgements

For Betty and Albert Bailey, two of the coolest people I know.

Contents

RUBEN KANE, forty-two, is a black detective who lives in Cleveland, Ohio during the 1930s and early 1940s. He's at the top of his game, known for taking cases no one else will. Tough, controversial, and dangerous, Kane is not your average dick; at five foot eight, 180 pounds, he's smaller than most but with no less heart. His motto is "Leave it to Kane; he goes further."

Dear Client   A Ruben Kane novel

Cleveland Ohio

October 20, 1938

The Montane building, thirteenth floor, office of Ruben Kane.

Chapter 1

DEAR CLIENT

DEAR CLIENT, I'm writing you in reference to our earlier conversation of 11/01/38. Here is a rundown of my findings from 11/02/38, the date you hired me, till 11/18/38, the date I closed your case. (Of course, you understand I didn't tell him everything, just the parts that pertain to him.) The lady you hired me to find was Miss Dolores Grace, age twenty-six, white, five foot four, 125 pounds, black hair, black eyes. Loves associating with Negroes and is known to be bisexual. Been missing for eight months. You contacted the police, but you think since she loves to hang around Negroes, they are in no hurry to find her. The family has lost interest in her and doesn't care if she comes back or not. You wish to remain anonymous for reasons of your own, but did send me a retainer by messenger. You told me some of the areas she hung out in and who you think a few of her friends were. You searched as much as possible, but being white yourself and new to the area, didn't get very far. So you hired me, and I started from there.

I buzzed Rita on the intercom and told her to get me Raymond on the phone. Rita is my secretary and has been working for me for a couple of years now. Of Mexican descent, she came to this country illegally. How she made it up to Cleveland I don't know, and she never said. Anyway, she needed a job, and I needed a secretary. Rita is five foot two, 250 pounds, long black hair, and carries a stiletto in her bosom. For a big woman, she is very light on her feet, as the guy she carved up here in the office can attest. After Rita got Raymond for me, I started asking him about the lady in question. Raymond is a barber in town you go to if you need a haircut or information, for a price, that is. Raymond has been cutting hair for over thirty years. At age sixty-three, he's still a big sucker—six foot four, 300 pounds, mostly fat now, with a potbelly, but there was a time. Three quarters bald with a clean shaven face, with those bifocal glasses he wears. Wearing a white smock, he looks just like a typical barber.

"Have you seen or heard of this lady, Raymond? I know you hear everything."

"RK, the kind of woman you speak of are 'round here all the time, there seems to be more and more white girls hanging around us (Negroes); even the white guys. I don't know what it is. Once they find out all the hell we going through, they'll stay where they are. Anyway, to answer your question, I think I have heard of her, but the girls I'm thinking of have really hooked in with a bad crowd. Robbing, drinking, drugs, doing it all."

"Any idea where they hang out?"

"I don't, RK, but if you talk to Little Jimmy he should be able to put you on the right path; that's the kind of bullshit he's into. Last I heard, he was staying in those apartments off Hastings and Eighty-Second Street."

"Thanks, Raymond. I owe you."

"Yes, you do, RK. Yes, you do."

My next move was to find Little Jimmy, but first things first—Skippy's Diner for lunch. Skippy's was an old railroad car they made into a diner; been there for years. Chicken fried steak, mashed potatoes, salad, and iced tea. Nice! Can't beat Skippy's for a good meal. After I left Skippy's, I ran into Frey, the shoeshine boy, just as I was about to get in my car.

"RK, what's up? Haven't seen you in a while."

"I'm still here, Frey; doing the same old thing."

"I know; I've been reading about you in the newspaper from time to time. You big time now, RK. It's a wonder you even got time to talk to an old shoeshine boy like me."

"Don't be like that, Frey. I never forget my friends. Since I ran into you, maybe you can help me." I went on to tell him about the girl I was searching for.

"RK, I know of a white chick like that, but from what I hear, it's not like she's following a crowd that put her in the shit. From what I understand, she's leading the pack."

"First I heard of that, Frey. Never heard of a white girl leading a bunch of Negroes; got to be a new first."

"I don't know, RK. I seen the girl from a distance, and I don't think she's white at all. She looks more like Arabian or Arabic or something like that. My observations, anyway."

I found Little Jimmy's place, and as I was about to knock on his door, he opened it and was saying, "Move on, bitch. I didn't tell you to come back in the first place. You only come back for the dick.

Well, I ain't given up no mo.' dick—to you, anyway. So you can just hit the road."

"Jimmy, what's up? You still having woman trouble, I see."

"Not after I get rid of this bitch. I'm swearing off women after this one and right after I knock off this fine mama coming over tonight. What brings you this way, RK? Lost? Just a minute, RK"

He went back to talking to the woman. "And take that goddamn cat with you, stinking mother jump. You were saying, RK?"

"Is this a good time, Jimmy? Seems like you have your hands full."

"I'm doing cleanup right now; it'll be all right." His lady came out the door, cat in one arm and purse on the other, saw me, put her nose in the air, and walked past without saying a word. I can understand why. Jimmy walked into the apartment, grabbed a bag she'd left, and tossed it down the stairs after her. "Come on in, RK; can I get you a drink?"

Chapter 2

JIMMY

JIMMY HAD IT all. Beer, scotch, bourbon, and gin. I opted for the Jim Beam over ice with a little water. I sat on the couch and pulled a pet toy I had sat on out from under me. Jimmy took it, went to the open window, and tossed it out. "RK, never get hooked up with a woman who's got a pet; you come out second every time. Now let's start over, what are you doing in my neck of the woods? You big time now."

"You know what they say, Jimmy, you can take the Negro out the hood, but he just keeps coming back."

"I heard that," Jimmy said. "So how can I help you. I know this isn't a social call."

"No, I'm afraid not, Jimmy. I need some help in locating a white chick by the name of Dolores Grace. Five foot four,135 pounds, black hair, is known to hang around with us a lot, loves to party!"

"There's a lot of that going around these days, RK. I mean whites coming over to the dark side. Must be because they see where we're living so well. But yeah, I've heard of one particular white chick that's something else, even got some of the brothers working for her. Maybe that's the one you're looking for."

"Tell me something, Jimmy, how in the hell did a white girl get in a position to do all that; how did she convince the brothers?"

"Money, RK, money! First, it was just a party thing, sex, alcohol, and drugs. At some point, came to the realization all that costs money. She came up with the idea of prostitution. Not the traditional prostitution, but where the brothers were used as the hoes."

"What kind of shit is that Jimmy? I never heard of men being used as hoes before; enlighten me."

"Well it works like this, RK, the chick you call Dolores, the brothers call her Robin. She came up with the idea that she knew of a lot of ladies in her old neighborhood who have secretly wanted to be with a Negro, so she thought they could cash in on that. The brothers went along with it. Free drawls, and white at that, plus they'd be getting paid for it. Robin started working the other side of town on the QT, and before you knew it, they were in business. They were given' the women hookers a run for their money."

"How the hell do you know all this, Jimmy?"

"I'm in the know, RK. That's why you came to me, right? You know, she's really not white, she's Palestinian."

"I need another drink behind hearing all this."

"Help yourself, RK. Hey, and that's not all, the word got around so now some men are trying to get a taste, white dudes. But you know the brothers stopped there, the joint (dick) they said is for the women, not the men. But then again," Jimmy said, "if the money is right, they may go for it. I believe a few did anyway. Answer me this, RK, are you looking for Robin to take her back home to her people? Because I'll tell you there is too much money involved now, she's not going anyplace."

"Jimmy, tell me this, what are the ages of these women?"

"I'd say between thirty-five and eighty years old, and what I hear is the pay is excellent. She only has about seven guys and two girls right now."

"Two girls?"

"Yeah, for those women that love other women. She's a regular madam."

"What's the play, Jimmy? I mean, how does she go about all this?"

"Goddamn, RK, haven't I told you enough? And you haven't said anything about our good white presidents. Can I hear it for Jackson, Lincoln, or Hamilton?"

I reached in my back pocket, pulled out my wallet, and retrieved two Jacksons. I gave them to him, and he smiled.

"What else did you want to know? Oh yeah, about their setup. First of all, she had the brothers pose naked for all kinds of pictures, in all sorts of dress. She doesn't give Theo's to her clients, but lets them have a look see. In turn, the clients would pick the one they want, and they go from there."

"Where does all this take place?"

"They have a mansion on the outskirts of town, but all the action doesn't happen there, they have it set up like a food take-out, or should I say home delivery. The married ones go to the mansion, but the single ones have their own place, and Robin's people go there. Check this, RK, since this is a white neighborhood, they have the guys dress up like delivery people. That's all I got, RK; hope it's worth the money."

"You sure have enlightened me, Jimmy. You gave me a little more information than I think I needed."

"There is one other thing, RK. You can't just go there and knock on the door and they let you in. No, you can't do that. They have people guarding the grounds, which are surrounded by a fence, and the entrance has a large metal gate. The insides have a few old boys lingering around, doubling as guards. If you want to see Robin, you have to make an appointment."

"Can you arrange that for me, Jimmy?"

"I'll try, RK. But it'll cost you."

"When can you let me know?"

"Give me a couple of days; I'll call you."

"One other thing, Jimmy. You never thought about offering your services out to Robin? After all, you do love to play."

"Hell no, RK. I think more of myself than that. I know I'm a dog, but there's some things even a dog won't do."

At the mansion, Robin was maintaining and coordinating her appointments. She was on the phone with Mrs. Corley, the sixty-two-year-old, short, heavyset wife of the CEO of Corley's Electric Company.

Mrs. Corley was saying, "Now, Robin, I want to change. The last one I had was nice, but he didn't have that oomph I like in a man. I think I'd like to try the one everyone calls Snake. I think he may fit the bill. Is it true what they say about him?"

"What have you heard, Mrs. Corley?"

"I don't like to say over the phone, but you know, that he can really go a long time and he has a penis over eighteen inches long."

"Well, you saw the pictures, Mrs. Corley, what do you think? Pictures don't lie!"

"Yes, that's true," Mrs. Corley said. "I do believe in pictures. And the other ladies were more than pleased with him."

"You do know that Snake comes at a premium because of his high demand?"

"Yes, I understand that, and I'm willing to pay. Is he free Thursday afternoon?"

"Hold on a minute, Mrs. Corley, while I check my ledger. Yes, he is free. Shall we say about 2 p.m.?"

"That's fine, Robin; I'll be there."

Robin called Snake and told him of the appointment. "You OK on your fly?"

"Yeah, I'm OK Robin. You keeping me pretty busy."

"Mo' money, mo.' money, Snake."

"I'm not complaining', you understand. As long as you keep hitting me up with that fly, I'm OK." The fly Snake was talking about was Spanish fly, a drug used on horses when they mate. Makes the males get an erection, and bingo. Men learned about fly and started using it themselves. Robin has the stuff shipped in from Mexico. She gave it to her people in injections just before they entered the room with the clients. The ones that go to the clients' homes inject themselves there. Robin is looking into getting the fly locally, for the right price.

Snake is her hottest seller, with that long-ass rod he has. Some say that thing reaches twenty-five inches when he's hard. They say very few of the local girls would mess with him because he's so large, but her clients seem to like it. She has a feeling that with that rod of Snake's and the fly, he's going to hurt somebody one day. No problems with the other guys; there're just average, but what's average for a black man is more than average for a white man. She hasn't tried Snake yet herself; could it be that she's afraid? Hell no!

The business is doing great; she may have to hire more women, but especially more men. Lately, she's had women call her from out of town. She may have to open up a franchise. Received a call from Little Jimmy, who wanted her to see some guy named Ruben Kane. She owes it to Jimmy, so she agreed. Kane was due to show up that next day, Wednesday, at two. She has to be sure to notify the guards or they won't let him in the gate. *Been trying to hire Little Jimmy, but can't seem to reel him in. I don't know why not; he's nothing but a whore his self. He's fucking anything and everything in sight; my way, he'll at least be making money. Oh well, back to the books.*

Wednesday 10 a.m.
"RK, Little Jimmy is on line one," Rita said.

I picked up the line and said, "Jimmy, you up early aren't you; good news I hope?"

"Yeah, RK, you are to meet Robin today at two. I would have called you earlier, but I've been in a poker game and just got in. I haven't even been to bed yet. Anyway, she said she'll meet with you for a minute; it'll be at the mansion. Next time you see me, throw a few of those Jacksons my way. Take care, and good luck, RK."

One hurdle down, now to see what Ms. Grace a.k.a. Robin has to say.

"RK," Rita asked, "has Ella returned home yet?"

"No, Rita, she hasn't. And I don't expect her to." Ella was my wife for a number of years, and we both had been going our separate ways but still living under the same roof. One of us would leave one day, but the price was right, so we stayed where we were. One night, I came home and there was a note on the kitchen table saying she'd had it and was out of there, or words to that effect. "Why did you bring up Ella?" I asked.

"Oh, I don't know, I just got to thinking about her. I liked Ella, she was all right."

"Well, I liked her too, but!"

Chapter 3

ROBIN

BEFORE I WENT to my appointment with Robin, I stopped by the service station to gas up the Buick. I noticed the petrol hadn't gotten any cheaper, still nineteen cents a gallon. Should be a law, this shit being this high. The attendant said that in a few years, it'll be as high as twenty-eight cents a gallon. "And guess what I heard, some fool has come up with the idea of selling water."

"Now that's crazy," I said. I paid for my gas, crying all the while, and headed over to Skippy's for lunch. I didn't know what I might run into at Robin's, but I sure as hell knew she wouldn't offer me lunch.

I pulled up to the main gate of the mansion at 1:50 p.m. I say main gate because Little Jimmy had told me about a rear gate that the married women go through. Looked like they were waiting for me—Mutt and Jeff, let's call them. One brother about six foot four, 180 pounds, looked like a totem pole, but was still intimidating (Mutt). Jeff was an inch shorter than me, fedora on his head, long-sleeved shirt with trousers up to his chest held by red suspenders. Now they were a sight. When Mutt walked up to the gate, I spoke to him from the driver's side window. "Ruben Kane to see Ms. Grace," I said.

Mutt and Jeff looked at each other and said, "Who?"

Then I regrouped and said, "Robin."

Mutt opened the gate, which was at least ten feet tall; one of those cast iron babies. Jeff had to help him.

"One day, we're going to have this thing so it will open electronically," Jeff said to Mutt.

Mutt told me where to park, and then he escorted me up to the big house, the mansion. Jeff stayed near the gate. The mansion had three floors; Robin was on the first, in what they called a parlor room. As I walked through the main entrance, I noticed stairs straight out of *Gone with the Wind* leading up and up and up. Matter of fact, the whole place goes back seventy-five years, with the chandeliers, statues of Napoleon and others, portraits of people, some I knew and some I didn't. The parlor was set up similarly. Were these people doing good? I'd say so. The parlor had a pool table, a bar with all kinds of booze behind it, a mirror behind that, two ten-foot couches, and three lounge chairs. Robin was sitting in one of those. I guess it was Robin, the only woman in the room. A woman who was approximately five foot four, nice shape, hair cut short and straight. Complexion more like that of a black woman than white. More like a Pakistani or someone from India. But surely not a Negro. It didn't take me long to understand how a number of us would follow her; she could go both ways, white or Negro.

"Ms. Grace, I'm so happy you gave me a few minutes of your time," I said.

"Call me Robin and I'll call you Ruben, OK?"

"Fine," I said.

"And what can I do for you, Ruben? I don't believe we've ever met. I'm sure I would have remembered, but I've heard the name somewhere. Maybe on the street or read it in the newspapers. But first, let me offer you something to drink; I am forgetting my manners. What will it be?"

"I'll have Jim Beam on the rocks if you have it."

After receiving my drink, I answered her questions. "You may have heard of me; after all, I've lived in Cleveland all my life, and I have been in the newspapers a number of times. You see, my profession is that of a detective, private, which brings me here to see you."

"And why would you want to see me? I'd guessed you're not here for pleasure. But then again, I am in that business."

"No, I'm not, Robin. I was hired to locate you by person or persons unknown."

"Now why would anyone want to find me? My family was glad to get rid of me. I was promised to a person back home, but by then, I had been Americanized and have no thoughts of going back there to kiss some man's ass, do his cleaning and housework, his bidding, and once he tires of me, bring another wife to the household. So you see, Ruben, there shouldn't be anyone out there who would want me back. This person who hired you, you have no idea who he is?"

"No, I don't Robin. He contacted me because I'm a Negro, I believe, and he couldn't find you himself in a black neighborhood.

So that tells me he is white or a foreigner. He paid me by sending cash through a messenger. I only talk to him by phone."

"Have you told him that you found me?" Robin asked. "And how much did he pay you?"

"He paid me three hundred up front, plus twenty-five dollars a day until I found you. And no, I haven't spoken to him since that first call. He's supposed to call me back in a week."

"Look, Ruben, I don't know who this person is who's trying to find me, but I'll tell you right now, I don't want to be found. How much would it take for you to forget you ever saw me?"

"Robin, I was hired to do a job, and my reputation would be on the line if I didn't deliver. Plus, it would be unethical, what you're asking me to do."

"Would five hundred do it?" she asked.

I thought about it for about a second, weighed the advantages of the three hundred versus the five hundred, and my answer was, "Would that be cash?"

Back at the office, I paid Rita two weeks' pay (ninety-eight fifty) and threw in a few dollars for a new outfit. Now, tell me I'm not a good boss! I called Bernie (my bookie) and informed him that I had his money and to send one of his boys over to pick it up. Meanwhile, I told him to put seventy-five cents on numbers 847 and 352 and also five dollars on Rainbow in the fifth to show. After that was done, I called Freda, my girlfriend, and invited her out to dinner. There was a new jazz group at the Ebony Club that night I wanted to see. Afterward, we could go back to her place for a nightcap and do the do.

A FEW DAYS later, I was sitting at my desk going over the mail and having my coffee when Raymond called. He wanted to know if I'd heard the latest.

"I don't hear what you hear, Raymond, but I'm sure you will tell me."

"Do you want to hear this or not, RK? Won't cost you a dime."

"Go ahead, Raymond, I'm listening."

"I don't know if you ever heard of this dude named Snake? He's known around the hood as having the longest and largest dick in town. The women duck him like the plague. He can hardly buy any pussy, and even then, he can never return. Somebody made reference to him going to John Hopkins Hospital and getting half that thing cut off; hell, that would still leave him with close to eight inches. Of course he never did go, but every now and then, he'll find some takers, those that's not in the know about him."

"Raymond, I guess you're leading up to something; what is it?"

"You just no fun, RK. OK I'll tell you. He was legging some old white lady and she ruptured inside; bled to death. He was taken to jail and is up on murder charges. I don't see how you couldn't have heard about that, it's all over town."

"I've got the paper right here in front of me, Raymond, and there is no mention of that."

"There wouldn't be, RK, because she's the wife of the CEO of Corley's Electric. Plus, you know the ones in the street hear it first. You may not ever see it in the papers."

"Where did they find her?"

"One of the flophouses downtown. Don't know what she was doing there with the kind of money she has."

"And how did they get hold of Snake?"

"He was leaving the room she was in when the cops spotted him. They were there raiding the room next door. They found Mrs. Corley in bed, bleeding like a pig, with her blood all over Snake's drawls and dick. His dick really got him in the shit this time."

Earlier that week, after Ruben had left the mansion Mrs. Corley had arrived for her appointment. Thirty minutes after Mrs. Corley and Snake entered the room on the third floor of the mansion, Snake came running down the stairs to the parlor, calling Robin's name.

"What is it, Snake? Aren't you supposed to be with Mrs. Corley?"

"That's what I came down here to tell you, Robin," Snake said, out of breath from running down the stairs. "Mrs. Corley, she's not responding, I think she's dead, Robin. I really think she's dead."

Robin ran up the stairs with Snake following, and when Robin got to the room, Mrs. Corley was spread out on the bed, bleeding profusely. Robin went over to her and felt for a pulse. She looked at Snake and asked, "Just what in the hell did you do to her?"

"Honest, Robin, I didn't do no more or less than I usually do. All I know is that after she saw my dick, she told me to give her everything I had. As she put it, 'the best you got,' and that's what I did. After I hit it a number of times, I heard a pop, and she went rigid and started to shake. The next thing I knew, she started hemorrhaging. She took a couple deep breaths, and that was it. I had jumped off her 'bout that time, not knowing what to do, so I ran downstairs to get you."

"Snake, run down to the gate and get Ron and Lloyd (a.k.a. Mutt and Jeff); tell them to get up here ASAP."

While Snake went to fetch Mutt and Jeff, Robin sat in one of the lounge chairs and looked at Mrs. Corley, wondering what to do next. By the time the boys got back, she had a pretty good idea of where to go from there.

When Mutt and Jeff ran into the room, both said, "Goddamn, what the fuck happened to her? Snake, don't tell us you did this shit. Is she dead?"

"She's dead," Robin said.

"Snake, your one bad ass; killed a bitch with your dick. I seen it all now."

"I didn't mean to kill her. Robin, I didn't mean to kill her."

"I believe you, Snake, but now we have to figure out what to do with the body. Having said that, I do have an idea. After dark, take the body to our downtown location, take it up to one of our rooms, and you two leave. Snake will tidy up. After you do that, Snake, you get the hell out of there."

Chapter 4

SNAKE

INTERROGATION ROOM NO. 3, Cleveland Police Department—Lieutenant Jeffries was interviewing James Woods, a.k.a. Snake.

"You do know why you're here, Mr. Woods, don't you?"

"No! You tell me."

"You're here for murder, Mr. Woods, murder."

"And who did I murder?" Snake asked.

"Mrs. Eleanor Corley."

"And how did I go about killing her?"

"We haven't determined that yet, but I'm sure right after the autopsy, you'll go down for the count."

"Well, until you determine that, I'll be on my way." Snake got up to leave, but the bracelet on his ankle that was attached to a ring bolted in the floor stopped him.

"Sit down, Mr. Woods. You're not going anyplace. You want to tell us how you murdered her and where you hid the murder weapon? We're going to find out anyway."

"I've got nothing to say Lieutenant, and I think I need a lawyer."

"Lawyer, my ass. Where you think you at? You won't be getting any lawyer until we find out what we want to know. We're gonna find out one way or another, so you need to start talking before we get busy on your ass."

Snake was never very brave, and he knew there wasn't a whole lot of pain he could take if they started in on him, so he's going to tell everything he knows. He'd try to keep Robin out of it, but you know how it is, one must look after one's own ass first.

"Let's try this again, Mr. Woods. You want to tell us again what you did to kill Mrs. Corley? Where's the weapon?"

Snake looked at the men in the room, thought for a minute, and said, "You won't believe it if I told you."

"Try us," Lieutenant Jeffries said.

"Well, OK, here goes. Mrs. Corley and I have had a relationship for some time now, and we were having sex and something went wrong inside her, I swear. Then she started bleeding, and I didn't know what to do. I was just about to call for an ambulance when you fellows saw me coming out the room. I was glad to see you, really."

"You expect us to believe that story, Mr. Woods? What do you take us for? Now tell us what did you use to make Mrs. Corley bleed like that, and don't tell me you two screwing did it."

"That's what I'm telling you, Lieutenant, dick! That's all I gave her, honest!"

"Bullshit," Lieutenant Jeffries said. "Who in the hell is going to believe that story? Certainly not us. Get him the hell out of here until we get the autopsy results back. Be ready to be cooked, Mr.

Woods. And by the way," he said to one of his men, "be sure to have him examined."

A few days later.

"Any word on Snake yet? They've had him a couple days now." Mutt was addressing Robin, who was in the parlor having bourbon out of a water glass.

"I sent our lawyer, and they claim he's not there. You know that's how they play games when they don't want a fellow found. They'll send him from precinct to precinct. What I'm worried about is Snake opening his mouth about our operation. What do you think, Mutt?" she asked. "You've known him the longest."

"He's been known to shoot off his mouth, especially if they put pressure on him. But then again, he's a good liar. He may tell them anything."

"I'll tell you what," Robin said. "To be on the safe side, let's head for the cabin. We're going to suspend operations for a while. Tell all our people to scatter, and we'll contact them when we resume operations."

"What about the clients?" Mutt asked.

"I'll call them and let them know we'll be out of business for a while and to call back in a few weeks. Meanwhile, I'll be cancelling the phone."

"How are we going to contact the clients once we get back?" Mutt asked.

"I'll just do what we did when we first started; no problem with getting back to where we were."

Meanwhile, Ruben's client called him. "Mr. Kane, have you made any progress on locating Dolores yet?"

"No, but I believe I'm getting close. Give me a few more days, and I may have something for you."

"That's fine, Mr. Kane. I'm leaving it in your hands."

"One thing I wanted to ask you that I never did."

"And what's that, Mr. Kane?"

"Why are you looking for her?"

"If you must know, Mr. Kane, she was promised to a gentleman in her homeland. She never arrived, so he is looking for her to try convincing her to go through with the marriage. I hope that answers your question."

"Yes, except that you never did give me your name, and why the secrecy?"

"You can call me Furan if that'll help, and I'm just a go-between for the family and Dolores."

"And where can I reach you when I find her?"

"As before, Mr. Kane, I'll call you," Furan said.

"Till then," Ruben replied.

Rita walked into the office with my coffee and said, "Lieutenant Jeffries is on line one."

"Lieutenant Jeffries," I said.

"Kane, how's it been going, my friend? I haven't heard from you in a while."

Lieutenant Jeffries and I had worked on a few cases together in the past, and I even got him that promotion to lieutenant. But he was never this friendly unless he needed my help, information, or both.

"This is a pleasant surprise. How can I help you Lieutenant?"

"OK, Kane, why you think I always want something when I call you? Why can't I just call to see how my old buddy's doing."

"Get off it, Lieutenant. What you want?"

"Since you put it that way, Kane, are you familiar with the Corley case? A lady found bleeding to death in a flophouse in the downtown area. Mrs. Eleanor Corley turns out to be the wife of the CEO of Corley's Electric Company. Now, we got the guy that we think killed her, but today, we got some disturbing news."

"And what's that, Lieutenant?"

"We got the autopsy back from the coroner, and they ruled her death an accident…by sex, you might say."

"You have to explain that one to me, Lieutenant. Death by sex, what's that mean? Never heard of that one before."

"OK, listen, we caught this old boy coming out of the murdered woman's room. We took him downtown to interview him. He said he never killed the woman, only had sex with her. He swears that's all he did. Something happened inside her while they were having sex, and she died. Now the damn coroner agrees with him. We took him through a physical, and I have to tell you, Kane, this guy has the biggest dick I ever saw. The closest thing to a donkey, I'd say. They brought in the whole staff to view him. The men were amazed, and the women moaned. Looks like we'll have to let him go, which don't sit well with the husband, Mr. Corley."

"So how can I help you, Lieutenant?"

"Against my better judgment, I'm afraid we may have to let him go, so I thought I'd call you to see what you knew about this guy. I know he's done something. So what you got, Kane, anything?"

"I'm sorry, Lieutenant, but I got nothing. Snake; I've heard the name, and what I've heard would do you no good. Snake is well known in the hood. Women stay away from him; it's very hard for him to get any pussy, and that includes from the hookers. I'd bet Mrs. Corley knew about him and took him on anyway. So, Lieutenant, you could say she was party to her own demise."

"Now don't start that shit, Kane. Her husband sure wouldn't want to hear that. There's nothing you can tell me?"

"Lieutenant, if I knew anything, I would surely tell you. I believe the old lady just wanted some dark chocolate, and took on more than she could handle."

"You can keep that to yourself, Kane. Wouldn't want that to get out. Look, I can only hold him for another forty-eight hours, then I'll have to cut him loose, and I hear his lawyer has been looking for him. You've got my number."

Chapter 5

ELLA'S NOTE

"RK," Rita said. "What you gonna do about the client? You already found the girl and been paid. What are you going to tell him when he calls back?"

"I'm just gonna tell him I can't find her or something like that. Or go over and see Robin again, and see if she can come up with something. Until then, I won't worry about it."

LATER ON THAT day, I stopped by Raymond's for a haircut and paid him the little change I owed him. Walked over to Bernie's place, played my numbers for that night and put a twenty on Shoelace in the fifth to win. Mama Sue's was next, to feed my gullet. Mama Sue's was the best soul food in town, an old house made into a diner that she'd been running for fifteen years. The thing about it is if you didn't know where it was, you'd pass it up. You find it by the cars in front. Greens, corn bread, ham hocks, and beans. She's got it all. In the mornings after the clubs close, you can't even get in the place. And if you're still hungry after that? Don't forget your okra, ham, and brisket, plus a roll. When I left, I was ready to lay down someplace. I headed for my apartment after Mama Sue's. I hadn't been there in a few days, and I needed to change my clothes and check my mail. Some mail had come to the apartment instead of the office. Since Ella left, I'd hired a cleaning lady, so when I went in the house, the place was in some kind of order, and all my drawls were washed and where they were supposed to be. Life wasn't this good when Ella was there and at her best. My housekeeper even kept my JB up to where it's supposed to be, even though I suspected she'd been hitting it now and then (Ella's never done that). Once she starts adding water to it, we'll have to have a little talk. After taking a shower and changing clothes, I walked into the kitchen, opened the cabinet, took out my bottle of JB, checked the level, grabbed myself a glass, and poured a large hit. Tasted like JB!

I sat down at the table and drank half the contents. My mind immediately went back to the day I found Ella's note on the table. It read something like this: "Ruben, it had to happen. You're not happy, and neither am I, so I'm out of here. I wish you well. Love, Ella."

Chapter 6

THE CAVE CLUB

I hate to say it, but for a second there, I had kind of a lump in my throat. We'd spent some good years together, but we just couldn't seem to get over that hump. I hope she finds happiness wherever she goes. After leaving the apartment, I headed for the Cave Club. A little early, but what the hell; anytime is JB time. Two or three drinks there at the house, it got to be boring and lonely. I needed to be around people. I stopped at a light and noticed a new Packard one car back and promised myself the next car I get will be a Packard. The Cave Club had a nice crowd for that time of the night, the club held about 150 people, but only around fifty were there. The bar was thirty to thirty-five feet long, with two bartenders. Around thirty tables, and right up front was a small stage. That night, there was a trio playing jazz. Piano, bass, and drums. I grabbed a seat at the bar, called the bartender over, and ordered a double JB. I had a few words with the waitress and asked her when could I get in them drawls again.

"When you had it, you didn't know what to do with it," she said.

"Honest," I said. "I'll do right next time. Give me another shot."

"Drink your drink, RK. You had your chance."

Damn, I said to myself, and smiled. Don't know what the hell I would have done if she took me up on my proposition. It's just the nature of the game; it never stops. I sit there another forty-five minutes nursing my drink, then a couple more, and getting into the music.

Jumper came up to me during intermission and said, "RK, I thought that was you."

"Yeah, Jumper, I just stopped in for a few hits and to catch this new group I've been hearing about. What you been into?"

"I recently got married. The wife and I have a one-year-old."

"Oh, it was like that, was it?"

"Yeah, you might say so. Look did Little Jimmy ever catch up with you? He's been looking for you."

"Well, he could have called the office, but then, I haven't been there most of the day. Did he say what he wanted?"

"No, he didn't; just to say if I run into you."

"I'll check him out, thanks." I left the club late that night, and thought it was too late to go to Little Jimmy's, so I made a point to see him the next day. As I was headed to the Buick, I passed that same Packard and said again, "That'll be my next automobile."

THE NEXT DAY at 10 a.m., Rita walked into the office and spotted me on the couch. She said, "RK, you back on that couch again? I thought you gave that up. After all, you do have a home."

"Well, Rita, I was headed home. Don't know how I ended up here."

"I think you drinking too much, RK. You need to watch that. Before you ask, I'm about to make the coffee now."

"Don't forget to put a little nip in it."

After reading the paper and going over my mail, I headed out for lunch. As I was about to get in the Buick, I noticed a small dent in the fender. Someone had to have hit me last night, I surmised.

Skippy's small steak and potatoes, salad, roll, and tea really hit the spot. Forty-five minutes later, I was headed for Little Jimmy's place. I had tried to call him earlier, but got a recording saying his phone had been disconnected. If I had to guess, I'd say Little Jimmy got busted in one of his poker games and was looking for that bread I owed him. But phone had been cut off? When I reached Jimmy's place, the door was partly open, and he was sitting on the couch with a bottle of Johnny Walker Red in his hand, drinking right out of the bottle. I walked in and asked him if he had another glass. It was only then that he looked up.

"Hey, RK, you got my message. There's a glass over on the bar. Maybe still a little JB over there for you; the Johnny Red is mine."

"I tried to call you, Jimmy, but the operator said your phone was disconnected."

All he said was, "Yeah! Didn't pay the bill."

"You want to tell me about it?"

"A heart flush versus four of a kind. That's what it came down to, RK, that last card. Largest pot I have ever seen; must've been at least five thousand in that pot." He took another hit out of the bottle. "I had my hearts on the fifth card, three up top and two in the hole, King high. He had one four card up top, so he must have had two in the hole. Damn, RK. I put everything I had on that last card, and I'll be damned if he didn't pull another four. Who would have known. Five thousand out the window, plus my watch, that was in the pot too. So if you have it, RK, I'd like to have those few coins you owe me and a small loan if you can manage it."

"No problem, Jimmy. Will five hundred do?"

"Yeah, that'll be fine, RK. Say, have you heard what happened to Snake?"

"No, what about him?"

"Somebody knocked him off just as he was about to leave jail. They say they cut his dick off and hung it on the day room bulletin board."

"No shit!" I said. "Where'd you hear that?"

"At the poker game. One of the fellows who just got released told us. Robin is going to be one mad ass. Snake was her heaviest earner."

"I need to talk to Robin. She still around since that incident with Snake?"

"She left town for a while, but once her lawyer told her that they couldn't hold Snake, I hear she's returned to the mansion."

"Has she heard about Snake yet?"

"I'm sure she has," Jimmy said.

An hour or so later, I left Little Jimmy's place, and as I was about to get into the Buick, I saw that same Packard again. Now, I can understand seeing the same vehicle twice, but not three times. I think, *somebody is following me*. I was going to see Robin, but I changed my mind. If someone was waiting for me to lead them to Robin, then they were mistaken. I stopped at a phone booth to call her, but her number had been disconnected too. I guess she didn't pay her bill either. Next, I stopped at a street vendor and bought a hot dog and a soda, grabbed my half pint of JB from under the seat, and sat there in the Buick on the corner, eating and drinking. The Packard was still about a half block away, so I decided to drive through the park and feed the pigeons. Forty-five minutes of that and I decided to head back to the office. The Packard followed.

Sometime later, Robin, Mutt, and Jeff had made it back to the mansion and started getting their affairs in order. Robin was saying, "I'll be damned. Snake has gone and gotten his self-killed. What the hell did he go and do that for? There goes a third of our revenue. Snake was one of a kind; never find another like him."

"Well," said Mutt, "we still have two thirds left, and that's no little bit of money. I think we'll do just fine. May have to put off retirement for a little longer. In the meanwhile, we have to get the gang back and start making some calls to let everyone know we back in business; minus Snake that is."

"Yeah," Jeff said. "Back in business. I may have to take Snake's place. After all, I like a little pussy every now and then myself. I don't even have to get paid for it."

"No," Robin said. "You couldn't take Snake's place if you tried. Besides, I need you right where you are, in case one of those husbands gets crazy and finds out about this location. As far as you getting a piece every now and then, we'll have to work something out. In the meantime, get out there on the gate and check it out. Also check the perimeter to see if anyone tried getting in here while we were gone. The place looks pretty good inside as far as I can see; the liquor is still here, anyway. Let's have a drink and toast to the coming business for the foreseeable future, and life without Snake."

That night, at the front gate, Mutt heard a pop and looked around to see where it came from. He looked toward Jeff and saw that he had fallen down and was on one knee. The pop sounded again, and it lifted Jeff off his knee and onto his back. Mutt dropped to one knee and pulled out his .45. When he heard the next pop, he grabbed at his neck with his left hand, still holding the .45 in his right. Blood was coming from his neck, and then the pop that he never heard tore the top of his head off.

Three men walked through the gate, all dressed in suits, and all dark skinned, but definitely not Negroes. One held a rifle mounted with a scope in his hands. The other two held handguns. They walked up to the mansion and to the parlor room, like they knew where they were going. They opened the door and walked in. There was Robin lying on the couch, gin and tonic in her hand.

Once she saw the men, she sat up and said, "Who the hell are you and what are you doing here? And where are my men?" She called out for Mutt, then Jeff.

"They won't be coming," the shorter of the three men said. "No one is coming."

Chapter 7

DOLORES GRACE

"DOLORES GRACE?" he said, looking at her.

"Who the hell is Dolores Grace? I don't know any Dolores Grace," Robin said.

And then he started speaking Farsi and she knew who they were.

First thing she thought about was that damned detective had sold her out. "Who sent you?"

"You know who sent us. Are you prepared for what's to come?"

"Look, if you're asking me to go back with you, that'll never happen. I'm staying right here in America. This is my home now."

"We didn't come here to take you back. You were promised to someone, and it was all arranged. You were paid to come back and fulfill that promise, but you never did. Now you have to pay for that."

"What the hell you talking about?" she said. "This is America. Get your asses out of here." She ran to the bar, where she had a weapon, but before she reached it, one of the men stopped her and grabbed both her wrists.

"Dolores Grace, or whatever you call yourself, the law is the law. We didn't come here to take you back, only part of you." He proceeded to reach behind himself and brought out the longest knife

Robin had ever seen—a sword really. She knew what they were going to do, and she was terrified. But of all the things she should have been thinking and praying about, all she thought about was Snake and how she never did get to lay up with him. Never did find out if she could have taken all that dick. C'est la vie.

A couple of days later, I received a call from Raymond, and he asked me had I heard about Little Jimmy? Before I answered, he went on to say, "Little Jimmy was found dead in his apartment, and it looked like he'd been tortured. He was still tied up when they found him with cuts all over his body, two or three fingers cut off, and one ear missing. They say he was really fucked up when they found him. I wonder why anyone would want to off Jimmy?"

"I don't know, Raymond. He had no money; he just got busted in a poker game and borrowed money from me."

"I don't know, RK, but it seems like Jimmy had some information and somebody wanted it."

I thanked Raymond and told him I'd see him for my next cut.

An hour later, Lieutenant Jeffries called and asked if I knew anything about the murder of Little Jimmy. I told the Lieutenant I knew Jimmy, but had no idea who would want to kill him. Then I told him I had seen him a few days before and about the poker game and lending him money.

"He wasn't a winner in the poker game, so it damn sure wasn't robbery."

Lieutenant Jeffries said, "No, I don't think so, either. He still had a couple hundred dollars in his wallet."

"Before I left, I gave him five hundred dollars, and to my knowledge, that's all he had. Was his phone on?"

"Yeah, his phone was on."

"So he must have taken part of the money I gave him and paid that; and he probably paid a couple of other debts he owed." I lied to the Lieutenant, or didn't tell him everything I knew about why I think Jimmy got knocked off, but right then I didn't want to say.

For the last couple of days, I'd been looking for that Packard, but it hadn't been there. I had been doing all the tricks I could think of to shake them, but then I noticed it was for naught; the Packard just wasn't there anymore. At first, I thought it was my client following me, trying to locate where Robin was. That's why I made it a point not to go over there. I'd wait till she got her phone back on and call her. Now I'd have to go over to Robin and talk to her about that situation, watching all the time for that Packard. So I still won't go straight over there. First I'd ride to the lake and then to the park. I wouldn't go until late that night. I'd go the back way into the mansion, and if I saw any sign of the Packard, I'm out of there.

I drove around to the back gate and found it open, so drove on in and parked, then walked to the front. The first body I spotted was Mutt, lying on the ground with a .45 in his hand, the top of his head blown off. Fifty yards from him was Jeff, two holes in him, lying in the fetal position. No weapon in his hand. *This don't look good at all,* I said to myself. So naturally, I patted both of them down for weapons. Jeff had a .38 just like mine. I took that and put it in my left coat pocket. Mutt had his .45, which I also took. Between them, they had close to two thousand dollars. I wasn't going to pass that up, so I took it too.

Then I focused on the house. The door was open, so with the .45 in one hand and my .38 in the other, I walked in and stepped to the inside of the foyer, then listened. I started walking toward the parlor and noticed blood drops on the floor leading toward the front door from the parlor. I opened the parlor door that was partly open anyway, took a quick look around, and saw no one other than the beautiful body of Robin lying by the couch, blood soaking the carpet beneath her. Her body, but no head!

Chapter 8

THE SLAUGHTER

I LOOKED AROUND further, but it seemed like whoever had done this was long gone. I headed up to Robin's bedroom to look around there. Maybe she left some coins around; you never know. What I found behind a picture was a safe that was partly open. All I saw was the cash, so I knew there had to be something else they wanted besides cash. That was all right with me; I took the cash myself. I left out the back and drove on out of there, stopped at a phone booth five miles down the road, and called the police. Reporting anonymously that there were three bodies, I gave the location. I didn't report Robin with no head; they'd find that out soon enough. I returned to my office, locked my doors, and took out the money and weapons. I started counting and came up with $18,750 from Robin's safe, plus close to $2,000 I got from Mutt and Jeff. I put the weapons and all but $400 in the safe in the floor underneath my desk, rolled the desk back, and took out my bottle of JB. Grabbing my coffee cup, minus the coffee, I filled it to the brim with straight JB, put my feet up on the desk as I glanced out the window, took a hit of the JB, and commenced trying to put it all together.

The client hired me to find a woman by the name of Dolores Grace. Found out later she was going by the name of Robin, the head of a male prostitution ring. To find her, I had to go through some of my contacts, one being Little Jimmy. He told me where Robin was staying and doing business; he also made me an appointment to meet up with her. After meeting her and telling her I had been hired to find her but the client never gave me his name nor why he wanted her found, she surmised it wasn't her family per se, but the person she was promised to; it was an arranged marriage.

She was really Iranian. She had gotten paid to go back, but never did, and she kept the money. She paid me three times the money my client did to forget I ever saw her, so I agreed! After I didn't find Ms. Grace a.k.a. Robin in the time my client thought I should, that's when I started noticing the Packard following me. I think I led them straight to Little Jimmy's, where they tortured and then killed him. Little Jimmy must have told them what they wanted to know, which was where they could find Robin. Tonight, I found Robin, Mutt, and Jeff, all dead. Robin minus her head. If I were to guess, I'd say they didn't want Robin back at all, they just wanted to prove a point. I've heard of countries not taking so kindly to arranged marriages that were not carried out. I've heard that even the girl's fathers, brothers, all relatives close to the family would go after the girl for doing something like that. For honor, they say.

But this is America, and they can keep that kind of stuff over there. In the meantime, four people have died because of it; so far, that is. I wonder if I'll ever hear from the client again. After all, I think he's gotten what he came here for, but someone's walking around with a severed head and will be on their way back to Iran.

They shouldn't be allowed to come here and act that way to one of ours, regardless of what she's done. It's just not right.

My client likes to be anonymous. I don't believe for a minute the name he gave me was his true name. So why can't I when I call Lieutenant Jeffries again. There's only so many planes leaving out of here for Chicago, and they should be fairly easy to spot. So I called anonymously. "The head you're looking for will be leaving the country soon. Look for Muslim men, at least three of them."

The next day, Lieutenant Jeffries called and I said, "Second call in a week now, Lieutenant. Where's all this love coming from? Don't you ever rest?"

"How can I rest, Kane, with all these dead bodies popping up everywhere? I'm surprised that you're not involved somewhere, somehow."

"Not me, Lieutenant. My business is slow."

Chapter 9

ONE HEAD FLYING

"YOU HEARD ABOUT Snake?"

"Yeah," I said. "Got to him just before he walked out of jail, so I been told. Any idea who did it?"

"Sure, we know. Now all we have to do is find out who paid him to do it."

"What was the idea with hanging his penis in the day room on the bulletin board?"

"From what he told us, that's what the person that ordered the hit wanted done."

"Any suspects?"

"I'm looking at the husband. Doubt we can prove it."

"I heard there were three bodies found outside of town. What's that all about?"

"Now, Kane, it'll take me hours to explain. The two guys we found outside must have been bodyguards. They were also robbed; no guns or money, anyway. The woman we found inside, without her head. She did have a nice set of pearl necklace and a diamond ring. We also found five thousand in a secret compartment in the bar."

"Damn!" I said. Missed that!"

"Yeah, they missed that, but upstairs, the safe's open and they took whatever was in there. We're thinking it's not your typical robbery due to the fact the girl's head is missing. Plus, we got an anonymous call talking about men from Iran or somewhere over there, and I guess they're taking the head back with them."

"What's up, Lieutenant?"

"What you mean, Kane?"

"You've sure given me a lot of information. What do you want?"

"Well, now that you mention it, I need you to look into these Iranian fellows, in case we miss them. I won't be able to pay you, but let's say I'll owe you one."

"Sure, Lieutenant, I can do that for you. I'll give you a call and let you know what I find."

Who am I bullshitting? The case should already be solved. I'd told him about the Muslims, all he had to do was follow through with that, and he'd find the killers of Robin, her people, and maybe even Little Jimmy.

But I thought I'd go over to the airport and look around so Lieutenant Jeffries and his men can see I'm on the job. I had Rita call the airport to get the schedules to Chicago, and then they would have to board another plane from there to Europe. She informed me that the next flight to Chicago was at two that afternoon.

I felt that they'd want to get out of town as soon as possible, especially with Robin's head in tow. I arrived at the airport at one thirty-five and started looking around. The only thing I knew about them was they were Muslims, but I did not know what they looked like. One thing I knew for sure, they knew what I looked like. I guessed I'd have to be bait. But no confrontation with them, and no trying to be a hero. Once I spotted them or they spotted me, I'd sound the alarm.

I sat in the boarding room lounge watching the passengers board the plane, but I saw no Muslims. The next departure wasn't until eleven that night. I sure didn't want to wait around that long, so I might have to go back to town, and that was a long drive.

Right before I was about to give up and they were closing the gate, three men came running down the hall, one carrying a square suitcase about four inches by four inches. I guessed just the right size for a head. About the time I spotted them, they saw me. There was no time to call Lieutenant Jeffries, and his men were nowhere in sight. I put my hand in my pocket, where I had my .38, and they in turn pulled what looked like a .45 and a Beretta. The shorter one with the case didn't pull out a weapon, depending on the two men with him to take me down.

I held my fire for fear of hitting bystanders. Too bad they didn't feel the same. For a minute there, it sounded like the Fourth of July. I ducked behind one row of chairs and eventually returned fire; what the hell. After firing at least four shots, I managed to hit one in the leg, and he dropped his weapon. Down the hall behind them, I saw Lieutenant Jeffries and four of his men running my way with their weapons out, firing at the three. The other Muslim I hadn't hit, they did, and it looked like he wasn't getting up after hitting the ground. The third dropped the case he was holding and ran toward the plane, went underneath, and across the runway. He stopped a follow-me truck and made the driver exit the vehicle, then drove away.

That was the last I saw of him until…

Chapter 10

RUBEN MEETS CLIENT

AFTER LIEUTENANT Jeffries gave me hell for firing my weapon in the crowded airport, I told him that he and his men did the same thing. He replied that they were the law and they could do that. Once he found the case with the head in it, his tune toward me changed.

Right then, he had solved the killing of three to four people. They weren't positive about Little Jimmy, but were pretty sure they killed him too. A few hours of answering questions, and I was released with instructions to report to CPD that next morning.

A BOLO was put out on the third killer. After seeing him, the cops had a pretty good description, and what they couldn't remember, I could. The one I shot in the arm was taken into custody. The other was taken to the morgue.

"Ten tomorrow morning, Kane. I'll be expecting you."

"Yeah, yeah," I said.

It was 7:30 p.m. when I got back to the office. Rita had long gone, and she left no messages. I walked over to my desk, took the .38 out of my pocket, put it in my top drawer, and took out my bottle of JB. Grabbing my coffee cup, I poured it half full, sat back in my chair, and put my feet on the desk. Only then did I feel relief in body and soul.

Well, I thought, *that went well*. The only thing for the Lieutenant to do now was to pick up the third shooter, and this case is over. The only bad side, and I did feel bad about it, is what happened to Little Jimmy. The others took their chances.

The next day, I made it down to Lieutenant Jeffries's office right after I went to Skippy's Diner for breakfast. I saw Frey, the shoeshine boy, and he tried engaging me in conversation. But I kept walking; the last time I'd talked to him, he'd started telling me stuff I really didn't need to know. I waved at him and drove off.

Lieutenant Jeffries had me sign a statement and asked me questions. Of course, most of the stuff I told him was bullshit, but he didn't have to know that, and he was satisfied with what I told him. I left there feeling damned good, especially thinking about the money I had in my safe. I even jumped up and clicked my heels together. I passed a homeless man on the way and he had his cup out with change jangling in it, asking for more. I reached in my pocket and retrieved seventy-five cents that I tossed in his cup; never let it be said that Ruben Kane doesn't care for his fellow man. I called Freda, my girlfriend, and invited her to go out to dinner that night. I told her I'd pick her up at eight.

At twelve thirty, I was back at the office, and Rita said, "RK, I'm going to take a late lunch. I've been here trying to clean this place up, and the time got away from me. So I'm out of here, see you in an hour. Oh, you'll have to get your own coffee."

I sat on the edge of the desk and looked out the window, thirteen floors to the park below, wondering if the people there were feeling as good as me. I'd never walked through that park, and I had been looking down on it for a few years now, or as long as I'd had that office. Maybe one day, I'd take Freda on a little walk through there. She'd like that. I must have sat there for twenty minutes or more, my mind all over the place.

When the outer door opened, the door between Rita's office and mine was partly closed and I couldn't see, so I called out, "Rita, is that you?"

I heard the outer door lock and in walked a fellow in a dark suit, black fedora, and in his hand was a long sword. The third shooter! "Mr. Kane, why couldn't you have left it alone; weren't you paid enough?"

"My client?" I said.

"Yes, I was. And you went over and above what I asked you to do. After finding Ms. Grace, why didn't you inform me and just leave it alone? Instead, after that, you had me doing it the hard way, following you around, getting the information from your friend. You caused a lot of trouble, Mr. Kane. Now you have to pay for that."

He advanced on me with that long-ass knife in his hand, saying, "I lost a head, but yours will have to do."

I reached in my desk drawer, pulled out the .38, pointed it at him, and fired. No sense fooling around. There was only one thing— where he should have had a hole in his chest, there was nothing. When the .38 should have had a bullet flying out of its barrel, there was only a click on an empty chamber. I had forgotten to reload. *This isn't good,* I thought. *Not good at all.*

As he reached the opposite side of the desk, he took a swing at me that hit the .38, and it went sailing across the room. He started to come around the desk, so naturally, I went around the other side. He swung at me again, and I jumped back. I grabbed the hat rack that was behind me and tried defending myself by thrusting it at him. I did that two or three times, and on that third time, he brought the sword down on my hat rack and cut it in half.

Now he was on my side of the desk, in front of the window. He took the desk by one end and tossed it aside. That sucker was stronger than he looked. Now nothing was between us but half of a hat rack. Since the exit door was behind me, I figured it would be a good time to run for it. I did make it to the door and unlocked it, but by that time, he was on me and swinging that sword at my head. I fell behind Rita's desk as he was about to swing again.

I grabbed Rita's chair and put it between the two of us, then got up, still holding the chair. And still swinging at me, he cut that chair to bits. Back in the office, with him chasing me and me backing up, I tripped over the other half of the hat rack. He stood over me swinging, and finally there was no more chair left. At that moment, with him heaving the sword over his head and about to come down on the real me, Rita came through the door and saw what was going on and what was about to happen.

She screamed like a woman out of a Boris Karloff movie, startling me, and sure as hell startling him. She ran at the shooter, all

250 pounds of her, and hit him so hard with her body that he dropped the sword and flew backward toward the plate glass window that overlooked the boulevard. He went through it to the street below, screaming all the way down.

Rita ran over to me and asked if I was all right. Aside from a few defensive wounds on my hands, I was OK. She helped me up and we both went over to the window and looked down. There he was, spread out on the sidewalk like a rag doll, with a few bystanders standing around him and pointing up.

After Lieutenant Jeffries had come, taken me through the paces and satisfied himself of my story of self-defense, acknowledging that the third shooter was the one who went out the window, he was happy. After cleaning up the place and calling a man to replace the window, I sat behind my desk and took out my bottle of JB. Rita walked in, sat down in the guest chair, and said, "Give me a hit of that."

Epilogue

I'm writing this letter more to myself than anyone else. After all, everyone is dead, including the client. So why *am* I writing this letter? Maybe to make myself feel better, I could have done things a little differently. Maybe Little Jimmy would still be alive; maybe Robin and her people would still be kicking. I don't know. All I really know for sure is my bank account is looking damned good, and that's a fact. That's what really matters.

The cases I've had—someone is always dying; can't get around it. Tonelli and Bullet, Smooth and his girls, Richard, my bad side, Ella's murder of her boyfriend, the meeting with Willow. And then there were the hookers and demise of their pimps. All of these had death surrounding them; too many deaths. Sometimes, I feel like giving it all up, but there's just one problem…I love it.

Yours truly,
Ruben Kane

Other books by this author:

Enlisted at 14…A Memoir
Enlisted at 14…And the Journey Continues
Enlisted at 14…Looking back

Willow…A novel
Willow…One for the Team
Willow…And the Medusa
Little Miss Willow…A Short Story
Assassin

Meet Ruben Kane
R.K. {Ruben Kane}
Ruben's Bag
Ruben's Bad Side
Smooth…A Ruben Kane Novel
Mo' Kane
And Then Some

Ducks in a Row
Just a Dream

Dream Catcher